Praise for th
Adventu

"Young wildlife conservationist and media darling Bindi Irwin, daughter of the late 'Crocodile Hunter' Steve Irwin, is as exuberant on the pages of this peppy early reader as she is on-screen...briskly paced and delivers its message with Bindi-worthy verve."

—*Publishers Weekly*

"Bindi's Wildlife Adventures series creates a wonderful blend of adventure, suspense, and wildlife conservation...Children who love learning about animals and who are as devoted to saving them as Bindi and her family are will love this story and the direction of the series—a fun and educational alternative to traditional animal stories."

—*New York Review of Books*

"A call to action for fellow 'Wildlife Warriors,' this light and fluffy tale in the Bindi Wildlife Adventures series might appeal to those who enjoy Ben Baglio's Animal Ark and Dolphin Diaries books."

—*Booklist*

"In Bindi's exciting series of books, she and her friends go on adventures in a variety of places, from right at the Australia Zoo to South Africa! I recommend these books for kids ages 6 and up, especially those who love animals and want to help them."

—*Amazing Kids! Magazine*

"*Bushfire!* is a great addition to the Bindi Wildlife Adventures series...The story is interesting and slightly suspenseful, really pulling on the heartstrings and propelling us into wanting to help animals in need."

—*New York Journal of Books*

"I have one son who is an avid reader and read both [*Trouble and the Zoo* and *Rescue!*] in one sitting. He LOVED them! Another son started reading one of them and is enjoying it as well...Now our eight-year-old daughter wants to read them too... So looks like these books were a hit in our house!"

—*Laura Williams' Musings*

BOOK
6

ROAR!

ROAR!

Bindi Irwin
with Jess Black

 sourcebooks
jabberwocky

Copyright © Australia Zoo 2010
Cover photograph © Australia Zoo
Cover and internal design by Christabella Designs
Cover and internal design © 2011 Sourcebooks, Inc.

Published by Sourcebooks Jabberwocky, an imprint of Sourcebooks, Inc.
P.O. Box 4410, Naperville, Illinois 60567-4410
(630) 961-3900
Fax: (630) 961-2168
www.jabberwockykids.com

First published by Random House Australia in 2010.

Library of Congress Cataloging-in-Publication data is on file with the publisher.

Source of Production: Versa Press, East Peoria, Illinois, USA
Date of Production: September 2011
Run Number: 15861

Printed and bound in the United States of America.
VP 10 9 8 7 6 5 4 3 2 1

Dear Diary,

If you've never seen a tiger up close then you're really missing out. They are the most striking, powerful, and intelligent animals! But sadly, tigers are critically endangered. Did you know there are less than 500 Sumatran tigers left in the world? We are really lucky to have three new tiger cubs from Sumatra at Australia Zoo. When we traveled to Indonesia to bring them home, we got tangled up with illegal poachers, the logging industry, and the hot and humid Sumatran jungle.

Fly with me to Sumatra and I'll tell you all about it.

Bindi

CHAPTER ONE

Bindi could hardly contain her excitement. She shifted uncomfortably in the back of the taxi. She had a very bad case of the wriggles.

Why was it that just when you wanted something really badly, time seemed to move in slow motion?

Right now Bindi, Robert, and Terri were stuck in a taxi going at about the slowest pace possible.

"Is the traffic always this bad in Sumatra?" asked Bindi, her face pressed up against the window of the taxi.

Terri shrugged. "It's my first time here, honey."

"I think we're actually moving backward," observed Robert as he stared at the traffic jam outside.

Terri gave Robert's leg a squeeze. "Just a little longer, kiddo."

Terri knew her kids were tired and couldn't wait for the journey to be over. Neither could she. It had been a long trip. Both Bindi and Robert were seasoned travelers, but they had already completed an international flight from Brisbane to Jakarta and then a domestic flight from Jakarta to Jambi.

The three Irwins looked out at the writhing mass of cars, bicycles, and general mayhem surrounding them. Boy, was it loud! The air was filled with the sound of hundreds of car horns beeping at once. It was going to be a really long drive.

Bindi willed the taxi to move faster. She had tried to explain to the taxi driver why they needed to move fast, but he didn't speak much English.

Bindi attempted to act out the reason for their visit, but she suspected he just thought she was a bit crazy. The growling and animal gestures probably hadn't helped matters.

"I don't think I can take much more of this," said Robert, his face pressed up to the window. He wanted to get out of the car and run. Kids just weren't meant to sit still for long periods of time, especially kids who were used to lots of action.

"Remember why we're here. I promise, it will be worth it," soothed Terri.

Finally the taxi made its way down less and less crowded streets before pulling to an abrupt halt outside a very ordinary-looking apartment block.

"Are we there, are we there yet, Mum?" Bindi turned to Terri in excitement.

"Are we there, are we there yet, Mum?" Robert mimicked his sister, equally excited.

"YES!" Terri grappled with the foreign currency and paid the driver. Everyone scrambled out of the car at once and piled onto the dirt road. The kids helped their mum collect the luggage. Standing before them was a concrete apartment block four stories high.

Terri checked the map. "This is definitely it." She looked around doubtfully. "I think."

"COME ON!" Bindi had one arm and Robert grabbed the other as they dragged Terri toward the entrance.

Terri knocked on the door numbered 3. It seemed like forever before they heard the sound of several padlocks clicking open.

"Goody, goody, goody!" cried Bindi, as she bounced up and down on the spot.

"Ssh." Terri held a finger up to her lips. "You'll frighten them." The door opened to reveal a young man dressed in khaki with curly dark hair and a beard.

"The Irwins!" Underneath the mass of facial hair beamed a large smile.

"Cameron!" cried a relieved Terri. "Good to see you."

"Are they here?" asked Bindi eagerly.

"They sure are, the little terrors. Running me off my feet!" There was a pause before Cameron realized that the family was politely waiting for him to move out of the way. "Hey, gang, meet the Irwins." Cameron stepped back from the door, allowing it to swing open.

Bindi, Robert, and Terri clambered up the steps and through the doorway. They couldn't wait to get inside!

CHAPTER TWO

Three very cute and fluffy tiger cubs tumbled across the floor to check out the new arrivals. With their big blue eyes and huge over-sized paws, the cubs were utterly gorgeous. For once, even Bindi and Robert were speechless.

"Aren't they beautiful?" asked Cameron.

Everyone nodded vigorously. Cameron stared down at the cubs with the same pride as any new father. After all, he'd been feeding these little ones their bottled formula around the clock for the past few weeks. Cameron ran the tiger enclosure back at Australia Zoo as well as being a trained veterinarian. He was an authority on all things tiger—they were his passion.

"Can we pet them?" asked Bindi. They were only twelve weeks old and still small. She wasn't sure whether they were safe to handle.

"Of course." Cameron knelt down to pick up the cub closest to him. "Be careful, they're a handful... especially that cheeky bloke." Cameron pointed to one of the cubs.

"Which one?" asked Robert.

"The one eating your backpack!" replied Cameron.

Robert turned to see one of the cubs gnawing on the strap of his bag. "Hey! Keep your paws off, fur ball." As Robert inspected the damage to his bag, an orange blur swatted it out of his grasp and pounced on the frayed strap.

"They do love to wrestle," noted Cameron.

"So do I," said Robert. He looked at the three bundles of mischief and sized them up.

Bindi giggled. "In the red corner we have the tiger trio and in the blue corner we have Robert Irwin, the Thunder from Down Under!"

Robert growled and leaped into the wrestling ring, followed closely by three pouncing tigers.

"It sure is good to finally be here," Terri said as she sank down into one of the wooden chairs against the wall. What they were doing was a world first. These three cubs would be coming back to Australia Zoo as part of a zoo exchange with Indonesia.

They were going to be the first tigers to come out of Sumatra since 1976!

Cameron sat down next to Terri, exhausted. "These three have me run ragged. I have to feed them every three hours or I don't hear the end of it!"

Terri laughed. "You're like a mum with triplets. Don't worry. Now that we're here we can set up a roster so we all take turns."

Bindi and Robert were now both rolling around on the floor with the cubs.

"Tigers are the best!" exclaimed Bindi.

As Cameron watched the fun, an

idea popped into his head. "There's a tiger protection patrol about to head out into the national park," he said. "One of the male tigers has disappeared from his home territory. They're worried about poachers and the tiger getting hurt. What do you say to Bindi joining me?"

Terri nodded. "Just try stopping her! Robert and I can look after the cubs."

Cameron asked, "Hey, Bindi, want to head out into the forest with me and see if we can spot a wild tiger?"

The expression on Bindi's face was answer enough.

CHAPTER THREE

Cameron and Bindi traveled in a rented jeep toward the Kerinci Seblat National Park. Bindi knew that the park was enormous and was the largest habitat for Sumatran tigers not held in captivity.

Cameron filled her in as he drove.

"This is a tough gig, Bindi. The tiger protection unit has their work cut out for them trying to track down poachers who set traps, illegal loggers who destroy the habitat, and even locals who use the land to plant crops illegally."

"Wow. Sounds like the unit is doing an amazing job!" Bindi was impressed. She stared into the landscape around her. Although they had driven only a short distance, it was obvious that there was a massive amount of land clearing going on in Sumatra.

"They chop down trees to make way for oil palm plantations," said Cameron. "Unfortunately, destroying the forests reduces the amount of habitat left for the tigers."

Bindi nodded sadly. The road grew more uneven as the jeep jostled and dipped on the rough surface. They finally pulled up next to two black four-wheel drives and a group of five men, all dressed in khaki. This was one of the national park's tiger protection patrols. Bindi was excited to meet them. To be part of the patrol you needed to be fit and have excellent survival skills in order to manage in the thick forest. And sometimes the people the patrol came up against could be dangerous. It was a tough job.

Cameron hopped out and approached the men. "Hello, everyone, this is my friend, Bindi," he said cheerfully. He signaled to Bindi to join him.

The unit leader, Sunya, smiled briefly in greeting but looked anxious. "We must hurry, Cameron and Bindi. We've had a tip-off that there is a group of poachers not far from here. It would be good to have you two on hand in case we come across an injured tiger."

Cameron nodded. "We'll follow along behind you." He wanted to catch the poachers in action, but he didn't want to expose Bindi to

20

any potential danger. Bindi gave Cameron the thumbs up. She wasn't the least bit scared of coming across a group of poachers.

"Ready when you are!" she exclaimed.

They set off on foot, the men walking quickly and silently. It was all Bindi could do to keep up. It was very humid and the thick tropical forest was dense and difficult to move through. It seemed to Bindi like they had been walking for a long time before the men finally gathered around an object on the ground. She moved in for a closer look. A wire snare was nestled in among the forest floor. The men studied the trap and broke into a discussion.

Cameron translated for Bindi. "They're saying that the trap has recently been used to catch an animal. You can see the spring has been pulled closed and there is tiger fur caught in the wire."

Bindi was horrified. "Is the tiger hurt?"

Cameron shrugged. "I hope not."

Sunya pointed to a nearby patch of dry dirt. "Fresh tracks."

The patrol moved off, following the tracks. Bindi couldn't believe they were now actually tracking poachers and a tiger. If the tiger *was* injured, they had to find it, and quickly.

CHAPTER FOUR

Now that they were tracking, the group moved more carefully. Bindi was certain everyone could hear her heart beating. She tried to calm herself by thinking about Terri and Robert playing with the cubs. Those little ones relied on her and the tiger protection unit risking their own safety in order to keep the tigers from harm.

Up ahead, the men came to an abrupt stop. They dropped to their knees and motioned for the others to do the same. Cameron and Bindi ducked to the ground. Bindi could hear the muffled sound of voices not far away. It must be the poachers!

Bindi and Cameron watched and waited. The men in the protection unit communicated using sign language. One by one they moved away silently, disappearing into the bushes.

"What's going to happen to the poachers?" whispered Bindi.

"If we catch them they'll be arrested and charged. Question is, what's happened to our poor tiger?"

As Cameron spoke, the patrol descended on three poachers in a clearing that was just visible to Bindi. She could see there was a scuffle and then watched as the three poachers tore away and ran off into the thick scrub. The members of the tiger protection patrol followed in hot pursuit.

Cameron and Bindi were alone. After a pause they both cautiously stood up and looked around.

Cameron led the way over to the clearing. "We need to find that—"

They both froze. Bindi heard it before she saw it. A low growl, which would be hard to mistake for anything else. She turned around very slowly. Facing her through a tangle of vines stood a very angry looking tiger.

"Holy guacamole!" Bindi yelped.

"Whatever you do, don't move." Cameron slowly made his way toward Bindi and placed himself between her and the tiger.

"What do we do now?" whispered Bindi.

"Hang on…" Cameron knew something wasn't right. He couldn't figure out why the tiger hadn't jumped at them or turned tail and run away.

Then it hit him. "He's in a cage."

Bindi gasped as Cameron moved toward the tiger. Sure enough, once he swept away the foliage, a steel cage was revealed. The tiger was trapped.

"That was close," squeaked Bindi.

Cameron nodded. He was hugely relieved to find the missing tiger in one piece.

"What would they have done with the tiger if they'd got away with him?" Bindi knew she wouldn't like the answer but she had to ask.

"Most likely he'd be killed and some of his bones and organs would be used to make Eastern medicine."

They both shuddered at the thought, staring in wonder at the majestic tiger, who continued to shake his tail and show his displeasure at being caged by giving another low growl. Bindi and Cameron could hear the rest of the unit making their way back through the foliage. They were drenched in sweat and out of breath, but they were also empty-handed. There were no poachers with them.

"What happened?" asked Bindi.

Sunya shook his head in frustration. "They were too fast for us and had a truck waiting for them. We tried to shoot out one of the back tires but only managed to put a few holes in the truck's door!"

Cameron shook his head. "What a shame. But the good news is—"

"Take a look at what they left behind!" Bindi pointed to the tiger.

The patrol crowded around the cage. Sunya nodded to Cameron. "We need to assess how long he's been caged, and if he's injured, hungry, or thirsty."

Sunya and Cameron inspected the tiger through the wire. It wasn't easy; this was no tame cub. Luckily, the tiger didn't appear to be injured, aside from having lost a few patches of fur on the snare.

"If an animal doesn't struggle, it can be caught relatively unharmed like this one was," commented Sunya. "It's when an animal is left caught in a snare for days and it struggles to free itself that the damage is done."

Sunya pulled out a collapsible water bowl from his pack and gave the tiger a drink. Then he turned to Bindi. "This is a good day. It's not often we get to release a live and uninjured tiger back into the wild!"

Bindi agreed. Surely a good day's work didn't get better than this.

CHAPTER FIVE

Meanwhile, Terri and Robert were beginning to feel as if their day would never end. Caring for three tiger cubs involved lots of hard work. They were constantly demanding to be fed and their bottles had to be made up by mixing a special formula.

Then, after feeding, came playtime. The cubs just loved attention and would do almost anything to get it. Even Robert, who always had lots of energy, was starting to feel as if he couldn't keep up. Thank goodness that after playing came sleep time. The tricky part was getting them all to rest at the same time!

When they finally got all the cubs down to sleep, Terri sighed. "Boy, I'm glad I never had triplets!"

"I'm bushed!" replied Robert. He'd never thought it possible to be all played out, but that's exactly how he felt. He collapsed onto the couch next to his mum. He looked over at the small bundles of tiger cubs fast asleep on their bed on the floor, feeling drowsy himself. Terri stifled a yawn and rubbed her eyes. Perhaps everyone could have a nap.

At that moment there was the rattle of a key being turned in the lock. Robert and Terri sat up, instantly wide awake again. Cameron and Bindi burst noisily into the room.

"You'll never guess what happened!" exclaimed an excited Bindi.

"SSSHHH!" Terri and Robert had leaped up and had their fingers pressed to their lips. "You'll wake them up!"

Cameron shrugged. "Too late."

They all turned to see three very wide awake cubs racing toward them. Terri and Robert groaned.

Playtime was on again!

CHAPTER SIX

The next morning, Cameron had arranged for Bindi to speak at the local school. They hoped to inspire the children to help the Sumatran tiger by explaining the causes for its possible extinction. Terri and Robert came too, along with the cuddly cubs.

The classroom was simple but very colorful. The children had been learning about tigers in preparation for Bindi's visit and the walls were covered with striking posters of tigers in their natural environment. Bindi stood up in front of the class while Cameron, Terri, and Robert stood to the side, holding the cubs.

"Over 80 percent of Sumatra's forest has already been destroyed." Bindi spoke slowly, as the children were learning English. Their spoken language was an Indonesian dialect called *Minangkabau*. She pointed to the colorful posters on the walls.

"What remains of the forest is

inside the national parks, which are protected. If you cut down the beautiful forest it means there is no home for the tigers. In the wild, tigers have less than a 50 percent survival rate anyway, and with less forest, there is not enough remaining territory for either the tigers or their prey to survive."

Bindi wandered over to one of the cubs and took him in her arms. "I've only been in Sumatra for a day but it's already been one big adventure! I was lucky enough to go out with one of the tiger protection units and we almost caught a gang of poachers who were trying to steal a tiger."

Bindi had the entire class capti-
vated. The kids stared, openmouthed
with wonder, as she described the
previous day's events.

A young boy raised his hand. "Yes,
Madi, go ahead," his teacher said.

"What happened, Bindi? Did you
catch the poachers?" Madi spoke
very good English. He was an alert
young boy the same age as Bindi. He
was neatly dressed in a white short-
sleeved shirt with blue shorts. Not
all of the children wore uniforms,
Bindi noticed.

Bindi shook her head sadly.
"No, Madi, we didn't. They had a
truck waiting for them and took off

before the patrol could catch up. But the good news is that we were able to release the tiger back into the wild, unharmed."

Bindi held up her cub. "Isn't he beautiful?"

Twenty-three heads nodded vigorously. The kids were all itching to play with the tigers.

Bindi continued. "The Sumatran tiger is now the last Indonesian tiger left alive. The Balinese and Javan tigers are extinct because of human interference. We don't want to lose the Sumatran tiger too. You all need to help keep the species alive. Will you do that?"

"Yes, yes, yes!" a chorus of enthusiastic voices filled the room. There was no doubt about it; these cuddly cubs were a hit!

It was almost lunchtime and the children were starting to get restless. So were the cubs. Robert was momentarily distracted by the thought of food when the cub he was holding wriggled from his arms and bound onto the floor. For a moment everyone was still as they watched the beautiful creature scampering across the room. Then they realized—the door was open!

Cameron was horrified. "Quick! We've got to catch him!"

Bindi and Madi were the fastest on their feet as they raced after the cub. He had already made his way onto the playground, which wasn't completely fenced off.

"We have to corner him by the gate over there," Bindi instructed. Madi held out both arms and waved madly, trying to encourage the cub to move in Bindi's direction.

"Here, little tiger, come on!" Bindi tried to coax him to her.

The cheeky little baby looked at them both with mischief in his eyes. As far as he was concerned, this was a fantastic game! He sprang to the side and raced past Madi. He disappeared into the bush next to the school.

"Quick!" Bindi and Madi were hot on his tail.

Cameron watched anxiously. He held back the other children from following. Too many people charging after the cub would frighten it.

Madi and Bindi continued to scamper after the cub, who darted this way and that as he explored his new surroundings. They passed through two backyards before entering a third property.

"This is my house," announced Madi, puffing like crazy. "Perhaps my family can help." He gave a low whistle and soon they were joined by his mother, father, and grandmother. "Help us catch this naughty tiger!" he cried. But before they could organize themselves, the tiger cub bound past them into the house.

Eventually, they managed to corner the cub in one of the bedrooms. He was finally starting to tire of the game. He took one look at the five people surrounding him and promptly collapsed on the carpet in the corner of the room. In no time at all, he was fast asleep.

"That was close!" Madi grinned.

"Thanks for your help," said

Bindi. "We'd be in heaps of trouble if we lost this guy." They all left the room, being careful to close the door behind them. As they made their way back through the house, Madi introduced Bindi to his family. Bindi looked out the window to see Cameron, Terri, and Robert racing up through the backyard.

"It's all good," said Bindi, calling out to them. "The naughty fella is fast asleep."

"Well done, kids!" said Cameron, pleased.

"Well done, Madi!" replied Bindi, turning to her new friend and smiling.

Madi was excited. "I want nothing more than to help the tigers," he said. "I would love to grow up to be a tiger protection ranger." He took a quick breath before adding, "Would you like to stay for lunch, Bindi? I have an hour break before I need to be back in school."

Madi's parents nodded in agreement. "We would be very honored if you would join us."

Bindi turned to Terri for permission. Her mum agreed. "That sounds fine. We can take the cubs back to the apartment. I'll come and pick you up afterward, Bindi."

After scooping up the sleeping

runaway, Cameron, Terri, and Robert each left with a sleeping cub safely in their arms.

Bindi was excited. She loved making new friends and was looking forward to having an authentic Sumatran meal.

CHAPTER SEVEN

While lunch was being prepared, Madi gave Bindi a quick tour of his home. His family raised their own chickens and grew vegetables in the lot next to the house. Bindi was impressed.

The aroma of mildly spicy food

wafted out to tempt the children back inside.

"Something smells awesome!" Bindi realized she was ravenous after her big morning at the school, not to mention running around after the tiger cub.

"We can go in through the front." Madi led the way down the drive-way, past a large yellow truck. Bindi couldn't help but notice that the back of the truck looked beaten up. It probably had more than a few logs fall onto it. Madi had told her that his dad worked for a timber mill.

They headed inside.

"Please sit." Madi's mother pointed

to a cushion on the floor. The whole family gathered around a low wooden table piled high with steaming goodness and soon everyone was eating with relish. There was rendang, meat simmering in spices and coconut milk, and lots of rice, along with karedok, a fresh salad, and some delicious green tea to wash it all down with. Bindi thought the combination of flavors was truly delicious.

Madi's father, Bashii, asked Bindi why she was visiting the school.

Between mouthfuls, Bindi explained. "I came to tell the school how the tiger's habitat is being destroyed by oil palm plantations, pulp forests, and logging, and that the tiger is also in danger from illegal poaching. If something isn't done, soon there will be no more tigers left in Sumatra. People should speak up about illegal activity instead of just letting it continue."

"We made these in school." Madi proudly held up one of his tiger posters. His family was very impressed, but Madi noticed that his father looked annoyed. As the family continued to eat, Bashii stood up. He turned to Bindi.

"This is all very well to draw pictures and play with tiger cubs, but I am a logger and this is how I put food on the table and feed my family. They rely on me to support them. If I lose my job then we will all go hungry."

Madi was embarrassed by his father's outburst. "But Bindi is only trying to say that we can make a difference."

"It is easy for Bindi to say this. She is a foreigner. She doesn't know what life is like for us here. The right thing is not always so easy to do!" Bashii abruptly turned and left the room.

"I'm so sorry!" said Bindi. She had somehow offended her host without meaning to.

Madi tried to reassure her. "It's

not your fault, Bindi. My father has a very stressful job and they are laying off lots of workers. He's worried he will lose his job."

Bindi nodded. Madi held out his poster to Bindi. "I'd like you to keep this so you remember there are people in Sumatra who want to save the tiger."

"Thanks, Madi, that's so nice of you." Bindi took the poster and stood up from the table, thanking the family for lunch. She turned back to Madi. "Would you mind waiting with me outside until my mum gets here?"

"Of course." The new friends

made their way outside and waited on the driveway.

Bindi looked at the truck in the driveway again. "Gosh, logging work must be rough. Check out the dents in your dad's truck."

Madi looked at the damage. "That's strange, I've never noticed them before and it's my job to clean it."

"What would cause holes like this?"

Madi shrugged. "Normally I'd say big logs but these look more like...bullet holes?" They inspected the dents more closely.

Suddenly, Bindi gasped and

then lowered her voice. "Madi, do you remember my story about the poachers and the tiger and how the getaway truck got shot at? Now your dad's truck has new bullet holes. Don't you think that's a strange coincidence?"

Madi looked offended. "What are you saying?"

"I don't know. I just think it's a bit strange and it might explain why your dad is so worried and upset."

Madi thought about what Bindi was saying. "What do you think we should do? Should I ask my father? He'll be leaving for work soon."

Bindi thought for a moment and

then shook her head. "We don't know if he's done anything wrong. I think we should follow your dad and see whether we can find anything out."

Madi looked upset. "I—I don't know…I guess once we know what's wrong we might be able to help."

At that moment, Bashii came outside. He didn't notice Madi and Bindi as he got inside the truck and started the engine.

"Now's our chance!" said Madi, making a split-second decision as he lifted the roller door and scrambled into the back of the truck.

"What about school?" whispered Bindi as she joined him.

"I'm top of my class," Madi whispered back, grinning. "I can miss an afternoon if it means helping my father."

The two friends held on tight as the truck reversed out of the driveway. Was this the right thing to do? Neither of them knew for certain, but they guessed they'd find out one way or another.

CHAPTER EIGHT

Bindi and Madi had their hands full just holding on as the truck hurtled this way and that down winding streets. It finally pulled up outside a large timber mill in an industrial area.

"This is where my dad works," whispered Madi.

They waited as Bashii turned off the ignition and locked the truck—but not the roller door—before making his way toward the factory. Three men were standing outside, smoking cigarettes and sipping strong coffee. Bindi and Madi peered out to see what was happening, while doing their best to remain out of sight.

One of the men called out to Bashii. He looked over at them but didn't look pleased to see them. They called to him again. This time it sounded more like a command than a request. As Bashii joined them, an argument broke out.

"That's strange," observed Madi.

"I know those men. They are friends of my father's. I don't know why he would argue with them."

Eventually, Bashii threw up his hands in exasperation and flung the keys to the truck on the ground. He stormed off toward the timber mill.

Madi turned to his friend. "I'm going to move closer to those men. We can't hear anything from here." Bindi moved to follow but he stopped her. "You don't understand the language anyway, Bindi. Stay here. I'll go."

Bindi watched as Madi crept out of the truck and shuffled his way down the street, hiding behind the wheels of the truck. He quickly dashed over to the next car and crouched down behind it. Now he was directly opposite to where the men were standing.

As Madi listened, he began to piece together the conversation. The men were arguing quietly and urgently about something, something that had failed, something they wanted to try again. In the end they all agreed on a plan.

Madi crept back to the truck to update Bindi on what he'd heard. Just as he jumped inside and closed the roller door, the three men strode toward the truck, piled into the front, and started the engine. Madi and Bindi were trapped!

Bashii, at the entrance to the factory, turned when he heard his truck starting up. Was that an arm poking out from under the roller door? To his horror, he saw Madi and Bindi waving frantically to him as the truck pulled away, down the street and out of sight.

CHAPTER NINE

Madi and Bindi watched as Bashii grew smaller and smaller in the distance, until finally they couldn't see him anymore.

Madi was scared. "I don't think these men will want us following them."

Bindi agreed. "Let's lay low and wait."

They stared out at the scenery flashing past. The truck was on the open road now. It would be too dangerous for them to try to jump out.

The truck jolted to a stop. Two of the men got out and walked toward a small house. As the two small friends peered through the back door of the truck, they were dismayed to see the men come out of the house carrying a large mesh cage.

Bindi turned to Madi. "Are you thinking what I'm thinking?"

"That cage looks about tiger size. That's what I'm thinking."

It dawned on Bindi that the men were going to put the cage in the back of the truck and that the two friends were going to be caught.

"Quick!" She grabbed an old blanket that lay crumpled on the floor. "We'll have to put this over us and hide." The children scrambled to the cabin end of the truck where crates were stacked in a corner. They sat perfectly still.

With much grunting and a little maneuvering, the men lifted the cage onto the slab and slid it right up next to where the kids were hiding.

"Oof!" Bindi felt very squashed as she pressed up against the wall.

She didn't know if she could keep still any longer. Luckily, the men seemed satisfied and closed the roller door.

"Are you okay?" whispered Bindi.

"Mmff," replied Madi.

Wherever they were going, it was going to be a squishy and uncomfortable ride to get there.

Cameron, Terri, and Robert were finally satisfied that the cubs were asleep when there was a loud, urgent knock on the apartment door. The cubs immediately woke, stood to attention, and began looking for mischief.

Terri sighed as she opened the door. "Is there no peace?"

She was surprised to see Bashii standing on the landing. "Hi, Bashii. I'm sorry I took so long. I was going to come and get Bindi once the cubs were asleep." She looked around for Bindi but could not see her. Bashii was on his own and looked deeply troubled.

"Is everything okay?"

Bashii shuffled his feet and stared at the ground.

"Can I come inside, Mrs. Irwin? I have something to tell you and we don't have much time."

Terri hastily stepped aside to let Bashii in. He nodded to Cameron and Robert and then cleared his throat. "I am not proud of what I have to say. I lent my truck to some men who blackmailed me. If I didn't help them I would lose my job. They wanted to use my truck for illegal purposes."

Cameron realized where this was leading. "Are these men the poachers we chased the other day?"

"Yes, I think so." Bashii went on to explain that that afternoon he had been forced, once again, to let them borrow the truck, not realizing Madi and Bindi were on board until it was too late.

Terri sprang into action. "Do you have any idea where they could be going?"

"I can only guess they are heading to the national park to catch a tiger. They will not be pleased if anyone gets in their way."

Terri shook her head. "Knowing Bindi, that's exactly what she'll try to do! Let's go!"

Robert jumped to his feet. "I'm coming too!"

Cameron joined them. "And I need to go because I know where the tiger is. But we can't leave the cubs..."

They all stared at the cute threesome playing on the floor.

They were too young to be left alone.

Terri decided. "Then they're coming too. There's a travel cage we can put them in if things get hairy."

Cameron, Terri, and Robert hurried outside, each with a cub in their arms and Bashii running alongside. They piled into Cameron's four-wheel drive.

Cameron handed Terri his phone. "I'll drive. Could you put a call in to the tiger protection unit? Hopefully the patrol will be nearby and able to reach Bindi and Madi in time!"

CHAPTER TEN

Bindi and Madi breathed a sigh of relief as the men trudged away into the national park, carrying the tiger cage. They hadn't been caught.

The truck was parked on a rough side road at the boundary of the national park.

"I don't know about you but I can't just sit here and do nothing." Bindi hopped down out of the truck.

Madi nodded. "Let's follow them!"

After walking for over an hour, the kids were exhausted and dehydrated. Bindi was also beginning to worry about how they would find their way back. It had been easy to follow the men as they tracked the tiger but, with no path to guide them, getting back to the town alone would be much harder.

The men slowed down as they reached a clearing. Bindi and Madi watched from a distance, hidden by the thick scrub.

The men looked frustrated. They had obviously been unable to find the tiger. Bindi felt like cheering. She and Madi stifled their happiness as they watched the men argue.

"Hopefully they'll give up now," whispered Bindi.

That's exactly what the men looked as though they would do...until they were interrupted by the growl of a certain male tiger who never forgot a face. He looked even more impressive than Bindi remembered. Madi drew a quick breath. The tiger was huge, with massive paws and sharp, shiny teeth. He let out a terrific growl that echoed through the humid rainforest. The men were terrified. They ran back, tripping over each other in their hurry to get away. But the tiger was chasing them.

One of the men reached inside his jacket and pulled out a gun.

"NO!" cried Bindi, standing up before she had time to think about what she was doing. Bindi's cry distracted the man with the gun. He turned to see where the noise had come from and at that exact moment, the tiger swung his great paw into the air and swatted the gun from the man's hand. It flew into the air and landed in the bushes, out of harm's way.

The two other poachers fled up a nearby tree in terror. The man who had held the gun crouched on the ground, petrified, staring at the tiger who stared back at him. The only defense left was the empty tiger cage. The man scrambled over, crawled inside, and locked himself in.

This seemed to please the tiger. He stopped growling and turned his majestic head to Bindi and Madi, who were standing stock still, close by. The kids held their breath as they locked eyes with a full grown wild tiger. With a flick of his long tail he dismissed them, striding gracefully into the forest and out of sight.

The children knew they had witnessed something extraordinary. The tiger had let them go.

"Wow," said Bindi.

"Double wow," agreed Madi.

CHAPTER ELEVEN

Before the two men in the tree could think about getting away, the tiger protection patrol arrived on the scene and were surprised by what they saw: two grown men cowering in a tree, one locked in a cage, and two eleven-year-olds looking in control of the situation.

"I don't know what's happened here," said Sunya, impressed, "but we have two honorary tiger protectors to add to our group." He shook their hands and handed the children bottles of water, which they gulped down gratefully.

"Actually, we had some help," explained Bindi. She proceeded to tell them all about the tiger. The patrol laughed.

Bindi protested. "But I'm telling the truth!"

Sunya patted Bindi on the shoulder, still chuckling. "Let's get you back to safety."

The patrol put the three poachers

in handcuffs and the whole group began heading toward the entrance to the park. It was a long walk to the cars, but Bindi was so looking forward to seeing her mum and Robert that she hardly noticed. When they reached the clearing where the vehicles were parked, she ran over and received a big hug from Terri and Robert.

Bashii was relieved to see that both Bindi and Madi were unharmed. He hugged his son.

One of the three poachers shouted at Bashii. He looked shaken.

"What did he say?" asked Bindi.

"He tells me I no longer have a job at the mill," explained Bashii.

Bindi shook her head. "I don't understand."

Bashii sighed. "These men are normally loggers, not poachers. Our boss put them up to this. The less tigers alive in the national park, the less need there is for a national park. No more tiger habitat. That means more trees can be cut down and we get more work."

They watched as the handcuffed men were bundled into a waiting four-wheel drive.

Cameron clapped Bashii on the back. "The police will sort them out. Hopefully they'll turn in their boss in too."

Bashii looked worried. "Come on, Madi. We must get home."

Bindi and Madi turned to each other. They didn't have the words to describe what they'd been through, but they knew they had shared an incredible moment even if no one else believed them about the tiger.

"It'll be our secret." Bindi winked at her new friend.

As Madi turned to follow his dad, Bindi handed him a folded-up piece of paper she had been carrying in her pocket.

It was the tiger poster he had drawn at school. It showed a magnificent tiger, not unlike the one they had just seen, living happily in the wild.

"Give it to your dad. He'll know what to do."

CHAPTER TWELVE

Three days later the tiger protection unit welcomed a new team member to their patrols. He was learning the ropes, doing a routine inspection of a section of the park. It was tough going in the jungle heat with a heavy pack on your back, but the new recruit was up for the job. After all, he had a very excited son at home, waiting to hear all his stories.

Bashii looked up as a special charter plane flew over the Kerinci Seblat National Park. He knew it carried the Irwins and their precious cargo. He waved at the plane before readjusting his pack and getting back to work.

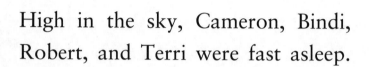

High in the sky, Cameron, Bindi, Robert, and Terri were fast asleep.

Lying opposite them in a furry huddle, three tiger cubs were also sleeping soundly. Sumatra had been a week full of adventure, and with these playful cubs there would be many more adventures—at home in Australia Zoo.

SUMATRAN TIGERS

🐾 The magnificent Sumatran tiger is found on the island of Sumatra (the world's sixth largest island) in Indonesia.

🐾 Tigers are the biggest of the Big Cats, but Sumatran tigers are the smallest of the tiger subspecies. Males weigh an average of 265 pounds, while females average 200 pounds.

- The stripes on tigers' fur serve as camouflage, breaking up their silhouette so they are less visible to prey.

- Tigers stalk and pounce because they are not able to chase prey for a long distance. Tigers do not have a lot of stamina because their strong, muscular physique weighs them down.

- With over 80 percent of Sumatra's forest already gone, the Sumatran tigers live in national parks. Their habitat ranges from lowlands to mountainous forests.

- The wild population of Sumatran tigers is estimated to be less than 500, making them critically endangered. The predominant threats to the existing population are illegal poaching and loss of habitat.

Kaitlyn, Bashii, and Meneki are the names of the original three tiger cubs that were the first to be exported out of Indonesia after a 30-year embargo. They were born on December 4, 2007, and arrived in Australia in March 2008.

Become a
Wildlife Warrior!

Find out how at
www.wildlifewarriors.org.au

Bindi says: "Don't support
companies that directly damage
the environment or support
activities that destroy habitat."

COLLECT THE SERIES!

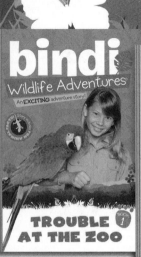

TROUBLE AT THE ZOO

BOOK 1

Bindi's birthday party at the zoo is going to be HUGE. Karaoke, animal rides, dancing contests—it's all going on! But when a spoiled ten-year-old boy decides he wants to take home one of the zoo's precious water dragons, Bindi, her brother Robert, and a green-winged macaw come to the rescue. Can Bindi save the water dragon and her party?

RESCUE!

Bindi and her friend, Hannah, are on a horse-riding trek in South Africa to see the amazing wildlife. While on their trip, the girls discover that a nature preserve for the giant sable antelope is being used for illegal hunting at night. When Bindi and Hannah try to help, they get caught spying. Will Bindi and Hannah get a chance to tell anyone what's going on and save the antelope?

BOOK 2

BUSHFIRE

BOOK 3

While on an early morning walk, Bindi and her best friend, Rosie, see smoke on the horizon. It's a terrible bushfire! As fire spreads across the national park, the girls know they must do something. They rush to the Australian Wildlife Hospital to help care for animals that were trapped in the fire. So many animals were hurt! Can they save a mama koala and her baby joey?

CAMOUFLAGE

Bindi and her family are visiting Singapore for the opening of a new reptile park. It's going to be so much fun! But when a rare Komodo dragon is missing, Bindi and her brother Robert have to blend into their surroundings to find her. Will they solve the mystery and save the beautiful lizard before the grand opening of the park?

A WHALE OF A TIME

BOOK 5

Bindi takes a pair of troublesome twins on a thrilling whale-watching trip. It's going great until one of the twins spots a bright flare in the sky. They race to the scene and find an oil spill! Can Bindi help stop the oil leak and save the nearby whales from danger?